Ethan and Oliver Adventures

A Thanksgiving Mission

A Thanksgiving Mission

Jennifer Zelt

For licensing inquiries, educational use, or permissions, contact:
Anchored Adventures Press
ethanandoliveradventures@gmail.com
ISBN: 978-1-969207-08-2

Dedication

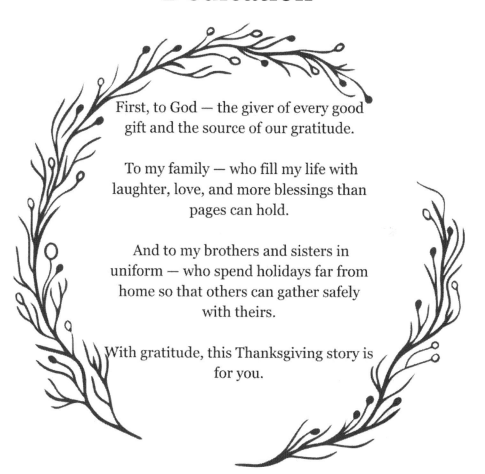

First, to God — the giver of every good
gift and the source of our gratitude.

To my family — who fill my life with
laughter, love, and more blessings than
pages can hold.

And to my brothers and sisters in
uniform — who spend holidays far from
home so that others can gather safely
with theirs.

With gratitude, this Thanksgiving story is
for you.

Meet the Adventurers

Ethan – Big brother. Thoughtful and curious. He is always asking big questions, sketching what he sees, and writing down the things he does not want to forget.

Oliver – Little brother. Wild and joyful. A question machine with endless energy, a big imagination, and a talent for turning anything into an adventure—especially if it involves climbing, splashing, or laughing too loud.

Mom – Retired Navy officer and the family's planner-in-chief. Once responsible for navigating ship movements across oceans, now she maps out each day's journey with purpose and care—connecting history, faith, and discovery.

Dad – Faith-filled storyteller, inventor, and history guru; and, a deeply involved member at their church. He manages everything from finances to facilities, and he can do it all remotely—so whether he is solving a budget problem or dreaming up his next big idea, he is always ready for adventure.

More Adventures Await!

Ethan & Oliver's journeys don't start and stop here!

Each book in the *Ethan & Oliver Adventures* series takes readers on a new mission filled with fun, faith, and family discovery.

Join Ethan & Oliver as they take a road trip through every state.

Every story blends real places with silly adventures, notebook prompts, and faith reflections that make learning feel like a family mission.

Collect them all and keep the adventure going!

Chapter 1: The Briefing

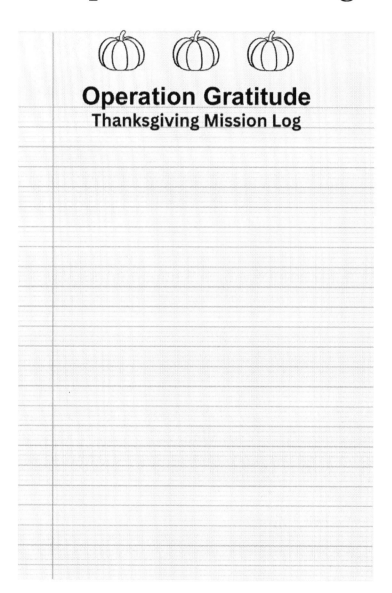

Operation Gratitude
Thanksgiving Mission Log

The November air slipped through the cracked kitchen window, cool and crisp against the warmth inside. On the counter, Mom's pumpkin pie diffuser puffed out sweet, spiced clouds—thick enough it felt like you could take a bite.

At the table, Ethan finished the last line of his math workbook with a careful flourish. Across from him, Oliver had turned handwriting practice into a masterpiece of chaos: a turkey with ninja arms doing cursive "g's."

"Oliver," Mom said, trying not to smile, "that is not how we make a capital G."

"It's gobble cursive," Oliver said proudly. "See? The turkey says 'g g gobble.' Educational."

Dad leaned on the counter, arms folded, peeking over Oliver's shoulder. "That turkey could probably bench press me."

From the corner, the sourdough starter made a wet blub blub BURP.

Oliver jumped a foot. "The bread monster lives!"

Ethan grinned, trying out a big word. "It's just the yeast and... microbial activity. Right, Mom? They eat, they toot, and the bread gets yummier."

Mom laughed, impressed. "Wow, you are correct!"

Oliver crossed his arms. "Well, I'm not eating anything that toots."

Everyone burst out laughing.

On the windowsill, three small pumpkins from their garden lined up like orange soldiers. Out back, the raised beds waited for one last tidy up before winter—carrot tops feathery, herbs a little sleepy, the soil cool and dark.

Mom clapped her hands once. "Alright, team. School is officially done for the day."

Oliver fist pumped and accidentally smeared graphite on his cheek.

"And now," Mom continued, dropping her voice to Navy serious, "we have a mission."

She flipped her planner around. Across the page, in bold block letters: **OPERATION GRATITUDE.**

Ethan straightened and opened his notebook to a clean page, writing the header like a captain preparing a log: *Thanksgiving Mission Log — Day 1.*

Oliver saluted with his pencil.

Mom's eyes twinkled. "Between now and Thanksgiving Day— just one week away—we're training our hearts to notice blessings—big ones, little ones, silly ones—everywhere we go."

"Do missions come with dessert?" Oliver asked.

"Only if you complete them," Dad said, lifting his coffee mug toward Mom. She tapped hers gently against his with a *clink.* "Pumpkin pie rations for high-achieving recruits."

Oliver gasped. "Wait—you mean we're rationing pie? Because if we don't, I will eat it all." He scribbled furiously:

Blessing #1 (Oliver): Pumpkin pie (future).

Ethan smirked. "That's why it's called a mission, Oliver. Plus I am going to complete the mission too—and I LOVE pumpkin pie!" He wrote carefully: *Blessing #1 (Ethan): Starting a new mission.*

Mom pointed around the room. "This starter bubbling on the counter. The pumpkins we grew. The fact that you two just worked hard and wrapped school without mutiny."

Ethan added:

Blessing #2: Our garden harvest.

Blessing #3: Finishing school strong.

Oliver scrawled:

Blessing #2: Bread monster (science).

Blessing #3: Pumpkins guarding the windowsill.

Dad's smile softened. "And blessings we don't always see. Like the men and women who are standing watch today—Sailors, Marines, Soldiers, Airmen—far from their families so the rest of us can be safe and free to sit at a table together."

"Don't forget the Coasties and Space Force and I'd even add all those who are first responders." Mom added in.

Oliver's pencil hovered. "Can I put them in my log?"

"That's one of the best entries you could make," Mom said.

Oliver wrote:

Blessing #4: People who keep us safe.

Ethan under lined his own line:

Blessing #4: Those serving away from home.

"Execute phase," Mom said, tapping the planner like a captain. "We'll do a quick garden sweep this afternoon before supper—pull the last carrots, snip the rosemary, tuck the beds in. Then dough duty."

Oliver gasped. "We get to punch the dough?"

"Gently," Mom said. "Bread. Is. Friend."

Out back, the garden beds rustled in the breeze. Ethan tugged a carrot and whooped when it slid free with a muddy orange grin.

Blessing #5: Pulling carrots fresh from the soil.

Oliver yanked one that came out the size of a pinky finger. "It's a baby!" he cried. "I'm naming him Sir Crunch-a-Lot." He chomped it in two bites. "RIP, Sir Crunch."

Blessing #5 (Oliver): Spy snack — Sir Crunch-a-Lot.

"Spy snack acquired," Ethan said. "Mission secure."

They snipped a bundle of rosemary ("for the potatoes," Dad said), brushed old leaves off the soil, and lined the last pumpkins along the path like a tiny parade.

Ethan paused, breathing in the chilly air, and wrote:

Blessing #6: November air that feels fresh and clean.

Oliver tried to march like a turkey and nearly tripped over his own feet. He scribbled:

Blessing #6 (Oliver): Turkey marching skills (needs work).

Back inside, the kitchen warmed up fast. Mom dusted the counter with flour; the sourdough sat like a sleepy cloud. Ethan washed his hands and took his place at the bowl, palms ready.

Blessing #7: Helping with the dough.

Oliver rolled up his sleeves and somehow rolled flour all over his face, too.

Blessing #7 (Oliver): Dough punching practice.

"Two hands," Mom coached. "Press, fold, turn. Nice and gentle."

Ethan felt the dough push back like a living thing under his fingers—stretchy, warm, promising. It reminded him of the garden: plant, water, wait, and then one day there's a carrot with a muddy grin.

Blessing #8: Bread rising like a miracle.

"Bread is weird," Oliver announced. "First it burps, then it squeaks, then you punch it, and then it turns into yummy rolls."

"That's called a miracle," Dad said. "Also called gluten."

Oliver replied, "Gluten tastes heroic."

Blessing #8 (Oliver): Gluten = hero fuel.

They set the dough to rise and wiped down the flour storm.

Mom held up her planner again. "Debrief time. Blessings you noticed today?"

Ethan read from his list: "Starting a mission. Our garden. Finishing school. People who stand the watch. Pulling carrots. November air. Helping with dough. Bread as a miracle."

Oliver grinned at his page: "Pumpkin pie future. Bread monster. Pumpkins on guard. People who keep us safe. Spy snack carrots. Turkey marching. Dough punching. Gluten hero fuel."

His voice dropped to a whisper. "I hope the people far away get pie, too."

Mom's eyes went soft. "Sometimes they do—sometimes it's not exactly pie, but something close. And we'll send them our thanks."

"Can we pray for them at supper?" Ethan asked.

"Absolutely, we will," Mom said. "Every night this week."

Oliver brightened. "Also, I'm thankful I invented turkey cursive."

"Show me again at the table," Dad said. "I want to see the lightning bolt speech bubbles."

As the first chill of evening pressed against the window, the kitchen glowed. The dough rose like a slow surprise. The pumpkins kept watch. The boys bumped shoulders and argued about whether a turkey could, in fact, do pushups.

Ethan scribbled what he thought was his last entry for the day: *Blessing #9: Laughing while we wait.*

Oliver added dramatically: *Blessing #9: Not turning into a pumpkin (yet).*

Mom kissed his floury head. "Deal, Lieutenant Pumpkin."

From the oven, the warm smell of roasted potatoes drifted through the room—salty, toasty, a hint of rosemary. The sourdough gave one more sleepy burp.

Both boys logged one last line before supper:

Blessing #10: Ending the day with family.

Blessing #10 (Oliver): Ending the day with pie dreams.

Operation Gratitude had begun.

Family Debrief

At the table tonight, share one blessing that made you laugh, one that made you think, and one you almost missed from your day today.

Accept the Mission

Start your own Thanksgiving Mission Log. List 3 blessings you noticed today—one ordinary (like bread or pencils), one person (a family member, teacher, or someone serving away from home), and one thing from nature (like a leaf, a cloud, or a garden carrot).

Faith Connection

Psalm 100:4 — *Enter his gates with thanksgiving and his courts with praise; give thanks to him and praise his name.*

Chapter 2: Roadside Reflections

The next morning, sunlight stretched across the backyard garden like golden ribbons. A cold dew kissed the grass, but the pumpkins still stood at attention along the fence line.

Dad had promised a quick drive to the farm stand after morning coffee, and the boys were already strapped into the truck, notebooks and pencils in their laps like junior mission officers.

"Checklist?" Dad asked, pretending to be the pilot of an enormous aircraft.

"Snacks—check," Ethan said, jotting:

Blessing #11: Snacks packed and ready.

"Mission logs—check," Oliver said, scribbling:

Blessing #11: A notebook that makes me feel official.

"Pumpkin pie money—double check!" Oliver added, holding up a crumpled five-dollar bill like a victory flag. He quickly added more:

Blessing #12: Seatbelt that doesn't strangle me.

Blessing #13: Snacks that crunch.

Blessing #14: Pencil sharp enough to sword fight.

Blessing #15: Pumpkin pie money (future pie security).

Mom laughed, climbing in with her travel mug of coffee. "That's supposed to be for apples, not dessert."

"But apples can become pie," Oliver reasoned. "It's called baking strategy."

He scrawled:

Blessing #16: Apples = secret pie ingredients.

Oliver stuffed a cookie in his mouth and tried to scribble the words, but his pencil smudged the page. "Ugh, too much writing," he groaned. "I need a shortcut."

He tapped his pencil like a bingo caller and grinned. "Instead of writing 'Blessing #' every time, I'm just calling it *B*—like bingo. B-17! B-18! B-19!"

Ethan gave him a slow head shake, though he was grinning. "You're ridiculous."

"Ridiculously efficient," Oliver said, already waving his notebook in the air.

The truck rumbled down the road, tires crunching over gravel before humming along the blacktop. The chilly air slipped in through the cracked windows, sharp and clean.

The road wound past bare trees and fields fading toward winter. A scarecrow leaned against a post, his hat flapping in the breeze. Cows chewed lazily in a pasture, steam puffing from their noses.

Oliver narrated every sight like a sportscaster.

"B-17: Cows making fog horns! B-18: Scarecrow with bad fashion sense! B-19: Barn roof shaped like a taco!"

Ethan pressed his forehead to the window, watching geese arc across the sky in a sharp V.

"Why do they always fly like that?" he asked.

"To save energy," Mom said. "The one in front breaks the wind, and the others follow in the draft. They take turns leading so no one gets too tired."

Ethan thought for a moment, then wrote:

Blessing #12: Geese who teach teamwork.

Oliver puffed out his cheeks. "Like when I have to walk in front of Ethan in the wind, and I get blown away first?"

Ethan grinned. "Except geese don't whine about it."

Oliver muttered as he scribbled:

B-20: Not being a goose. B-21: Tractor on the side of the road. B-22: Mud puddles shaped like dinosaurs. B-23: Road signs that don't boss me around. B-24: Clouds that look like mashed potatoes. B-25: Geese honking louder than Ethan.

Dad shook his head, smiling. "Your log's going to be full before we even get there."

The truck pulled into the farm stand, a cheerful shack with bright orange gourds stacked in crooked pyramids. A hand-painted sign read: Hot cider & pies inside. The air smelled like cinnamon and hay bales.

Oliver charged straight to the pie table, nose practically pressed to the glass. "Pumpkin! Apple! Pecan! How is a man supposed to choose?"

"You're eight," Ethan said. "Not a man."

"Eight is practically manhood when pie is involved," Oliver declared, scribbling:

B-26: Pecan pie (nutty happiness). B-27: Apple pie (fruity happiness). B-28: Pumpkin pie (eternal happiness). B-29: Pies that call my name.

He cupped his ear dramatically. "Did you hear that? The pumpkin one just said Oliverrrrr."

Mom picked out apples and a jug of cider while Dad paid for a bag of mixed gourds. The lady at the counter slipped two extra cookies into Oliver's hand with a wink.

Back outside, Ethan flipped open his notebook.

Blessing #13: Farm stands in the fall.

Blessing #14: Honest work that grows food.

Oliver stuffed another cookie in his mouth, "B-30! Free cookies! B-31! Friendly farm lady who understands my needs! B-32! Wooden floor that creaks like a ghost! B-33! Free toothpick samples!"

Ethan gave him a slow head shake, grinning despite himself.

"Ridiculously efficient," Oliver corrected, spraying crumbs as he wrote B-34 in giant, wobbly letters.

They loaded up and headed home, cider scent filling the truck. Ethan sipped and sighed. "This is my favorite kind of day. No school work. We're out together. It feels...thankful."

He wrote:

Blessing #15: Ordinary days that feel special.

Dad nodded, eyes on the road. "That's exactly what this mission is about, son. Learning to see blessings on ordinary days."

Oliver slurped dramatically from his cup. "Then put this down—" He raised his notebook like a bingo card.

B-35: Warm cider moustache. B-36: Burping cider bubbles. B-37: Cup that makes a funny slurp noise. B-38: Apple seeds I can plant into pie trees. B-39: Gourd that looks like a duck. B-40: Belly jiggles after cider.

He patted his stomach and made a ridiculous jiggle sound, setting everyone laughing until the truck rattled with joy.

Back home, they carried apples and gourds to the kitchen. Mom lined them on the counter while Ethan reviewed his mission log page with pride.

Blessing #16: Bringing harvest into the kitchen.

Oliver stacked three gourds into a snowman shape and stuck a carrot nose in the middle. "Meet Sir Gourdington the Third," he announced, bowing deeply.

B-41: Vegetable snowmen. B-42: Carrot noses. B-43: Gourds stacked like pancakes.

Mom shook her head, laughing. "Maybe not friends we'll keep long term."

But Ethan had already written it down, pencil scratching across the page: *Blessing #17: Laughing at Oliver's creations.*

23

Family Debrief

If you stopped at a roadside stand today, what would you be most thankful for—something to eat, something to see, or someone you met?

Faith Connection

James 1:17 — *Every good and perfect gift is from above, coming down from the Father of the heavenly lights.*

Chapter 3: History & Harvest

By Wednesday, the family's Operation Gratitude had collected a whole list of blessings: garden carrots, warm cider, pie (listed three separate times by Oliver), and even Sir Gourdington the Third, who was now slowly slumping on the kitchen counter.

"Mission update," Mom announced at breakfast. "Today we're taking this adventure on the road. Field trip—to Julian."

Oliver pumped his fist. "Yes! Best subject ever."

"What subject is that?" Ethan asked, raising an eyebrow.

"Snackology," Oliver said. "B-38!" He scribbled furiously.

B-38: Pancakes for breakfast. B-39: Field trips. B-40: Snackology is a real science.

Ethan rolled his eyes but smiled, writing carefully:

Blessing #17: Family road trips.

Mom smiled, sipping her coffee. "History—and how it connects to Thanksgiving."

The drive wound east through the mountains, the air turning cooler as the truck climbed higher. The road twisted and turned, lined with golden leaves clinging stubbornly to branches. Rocky cliffs gave way to valleys dotted with apple orchards, their bare branches stretching into the November sky.

Signs for fresh cider, homemade pie, and "U-pick apples" popped up along the road. A horse stood lazily behind a fence, swishing its tail. A hawk circled above, its cry sharp in the cold morning air.

Oliver pressed his nose to the window, narrating like a radio announcer.

"B-41: Mountains that make my ears pop. B-42: Clouds shaped like mashed potatoes again. B-43: Pie signs every five feet—proof God loves us. B-44: Horses with fancy tails. B-45: Hawks who yell at us from the sky."

Ethan chuckled and wrote:

Blessing #18: Autumn orchards.

Blessing #19: Morning light in the mountains.

Dad whistled low as the truck curved around another bend. "Pioneers would've crossed these mountains with wagons and oxen. No roads, no gas stations. Just determination."

Ethan pictured it and scribbled:

Blessing #20: Roads that make travel easier.

Oliver groaned dramatically. "B-46: Not having to walk up this mountain. B-47: Cars with heaters. B-48: Not being an ox."

Everyone laughed so hard the truck swerved slightly before Dad corrected it.

When they rolled into Julian, the little gold-rush town looked like something from a history book. Wooden storefronts leaned shoulder-to-shoulder, painted signs creaking gently in the breeze. The smell of cinnamon and woodsmoke drifted down Main Street.

Oliver pointed wildly. "B-49: Horses tied up outside a store! B-50: Cowboy hats on actual cowboys! B-51: Smell of pie in the whole town!"

Ethan stepped out of the truck, notebook in hand, eyes scanning the cabins just off the street. Their weathered logs looked gray and ancient, with a sign explaining how settlers had farmed the land. "It looks so empty."

"That's because life back then wasn't about stuff," Dad said. "It was about survival—food, shelter, family, faith."

Ethan nodded and added:

Blessing #21: Families who worked hard together.

Oliver pressed his nose against the glass of a tiny cabin. Inside, a rough wooden table held a few bowls and a cracked pitcher. "No TV? No video games? No pie display? Tragedy!"

He scribbled:

B-52: Surviving without TV (barely). B-53: Surviving without pie (impossible).

Ethan smirked. "They probably had one pie. For, like, the entire week."

Oliver clutched his stomach. "B-54: Not living in the Olden Days. Double tragedy avoided."

Mom knelt beside the boys, pointing toward the orchards in the distance. "The families here had to grow apples, raise chickens, and hunt for food. They had to pray the harvest was enough to last through winter. That's one reason Thanksgiving was so important—stopping to thank God for His provision, even when life was hard."

Ethan's pencil scratched across his page:

Blessing #22: Harvests that feed people.

Oliver added quickly:

B-55: Chickens. B-56: Eggs for breakfast. B-57: Drumsticks for dinner. B-58: Double win.

Dad chuckled. "You'd make a fine pioneer, Oliver."

"Nope," Oliver said. "Too few pies. B-59: Living right now, where pie is plentiful."

They wandered past another sign, this one about the very first harvest festival. Ethan read it out loud, slow and serious: "Despite a hard winter and many losses, they gave thanks to God for what they had."

The words sank in, quieting even Oliver for a moment.

Mom laid a hand on Ethan's shoulder. "See? Gratitude isn't just for easy days. It's for hard ones, too."

Ethan nodded and added one more line:

Blessing #23: Thankfulness even when things are tough.

Oliver peeked over and scrawled underneath:

B-60: Having a brother who does my reading for me.

Ethan groaned. "That doesn't count."

"Counts in Bingo," Oliver said with a grin. "Mission secure."

As they climbed back into the truck, the smell of fresh-baked apple pie drifted from the café on the corner. Steam fogged the windows, sweet and spiced.

Oliver sniffed dramatically. "B-61: Pie in the present tense. B-62: Pies in the future tense. B-63: Pies in every tense." He waved his notebook like a preacher. "Pies eternal!"

Mom laughed. "Maybe we'll make a stop on the way out of town."

Oliver's eyes went wide. "Double mission secure. B-64: Mom promising pie."

Dad started the engine as Main Street twinkled with lantern light. Ethan closed his notebook, satisfied. Oliver clutched his like a prize.

Operation Gratitude was rolling strong.

Notebook time!

If you lived in the "Olden Days," what's one thing you'd miss most? What's one blessing you think you'd still be thankful for?

Faith Connection

Psalm 136:1 — *Give thanks to the Lord, for he is good. His love endures forever.*

Chapter 4: The Gathering

By Wednesday afternoon the truck rolled up the long gravel driveway, the backseat smelled like a traveling bakery—cider, apples, and a suspicious amount of cookie crumbs (Oliver swore the farm lady gave him three).

Grandma swung open the screen door before they'd even parked. "There's my crew!" she called, arms wide. The smell of cinnamon and roasted turkey drifted out behind her like a parade float.

Oliver leapt from the truck and barreled up the steps, nearly knocking the screen door off its hinges. "Grandmaaaa! Do you have pie?"

Grandma laughed, hugging him tight. "Not yet. But I've got dough waiting."

"B-57: Grandma hugs. B-58: Grandma promising pie," Oliver announced, scribbling as fast as he could.

Ethan climbed the steps more carefully, setting the bag of apples on the porch. Grandpa came out with his old San Diego ballcap perched on his head and scooped Ethan into a bear hug. "Mission team reporting for duty!"

Ethan smiled and wrote neatly:

Blessing #22: Grandpa's bear hugs.

Inside, the kitchen was alive with clatter and warmth. Flour dusted the counters, a giant pumpkin pie cooled near the window, and a pot of cranberries bubbled with cheerful *pop-pop-pops.*

Oliver leaned over the cranberries, nose twitching. "They're alive. First the bread monster, now cranberry grenades." He jotted gleefully:

B-59: Cranberry grenades. B-60: Wooden spoons for defense. B-61: Cranberries that sound like fireworks.

Ethan snorted. "They're just popping."

He noted calmly:

Blessing #23: Cranberry sauce simmering.

Oliver shielded himself with a wooden spoon like a sword. "Defensive stance!"

Grandma handed Ethan an apron and pointed to a mound of sourdough waiting in a bowl. "You're on kneading duty, mister."

Ethan washed his hands and dug in, folding and pressing with practiced rhythm. The dough was stretchy and strong, alive under his palms. Grandma nodded approvingly. "You've got the hands of a baker."

Ethan smiled and wrote with sticky, doughy hands:
Blessing #24: Learning Grandma's recipes.

Oliver slapped at his own dough ball and sent flour snowing across the counter, into his hair, onto Grandpa's ballcap. "I'm a flour warrior!" he declared.

He scribbled across the page:

B-62: Flour tornado powers. B-63: Grandpa wearing flour. B-64: White hair upgrade.

"More like a flour tornado," Ethan said, brushing white streaks off his notebook.

Dad carried in a basket from the truck—carrots, rosemary, and the last of the garden pumpkins. "Operation Garden Transfer complete."

Grandpa clapped his hands. "Then it's time for my famous roasted carrots. Secret ingredient: butter. And more butter."

Oliver cheered and shouted:

B-65: Butter. B-66: More butter. B-67: Carrots that taste like candy.

While Ethan lined up carrots on a tray, Oliver tried carving a face into one of the garden pumpkins with a butter knife. "Behold! Pumpkin Pie Man, defender of desserts."

"Not my pie pumpkins!" Grandma gasped in mock horror.

"Don't worry," Oliver said. "He's volunteering as tribute." He logged it triumphantly:

B-68: Pumpkin Pie Man. B-69: Volunteer pumpkins.

The kitchen roared with laughter. Ethan carefully recorded: *Blessing #25: Family laughter filling the kitchen.*

By evening, the counters overflowed: sourdough rolls lined up in perfect rows, pumpkin pie cooling beside apple crisp, carrots glazed and shining like jewels. The whole house smelled like comfort and tradition.

Grandpa leaned back in his chair, watching the bustle. "You know, it's not just the food I'm grateful for. It's all this—family filling the kitchen. That's the real feast."

Mom smiled and tucked a stray hair behind her ear. "Exactly why we're on this mission. Noticing blessings like these."

Ethan wrote quickly in his log:

Blessing #26: Grandma's kitchen.

Blessing #27: The smell of home cooking.

Oliver added, with exaggerated swoops:

B-70: Pie cooling on the counter. B-71: Apple crisp calling my name. B-72: Kitchen clatter music. B-73: Grandpa's jokes. B-74: Sneaking cookie crumb #4.

As the sourdough rose in the oven, the family gathered in the living room. Outside, the November night wrapped the house in quiet. Inside, warmth, light, and laughter wrapped tighter still.

Ethan closed his notebook with care:

Blessing #28: Nights filled with family.

Oliver sprawled across the couch like a king. "*B-75: Couch snuggles. B-76: Family movie nights. B-77: Surviving cranberry grenades.*"

Ethan gave him a slow, fond head shake. "You're basically running your own Bingo game now."

Oliver grinned. "Exactly. And I'm winning."

Family Time Conversation

What's your favorite smell or sound when your family gathers? How does it remind you to be thankful?

Faith Connection

Colossians 3:15 — *Let the peace of Christ rule in your hearts, since as members of one body you were called to peace. And be thankful.*

Chapter 5: The Table

Thanksgiving morning smelled like heaven: roasted turkey, cinnamon, melted butter, and pumpkin pie all blending together in a delicious cloud that made Oliver practically float to the kitchen.

"Can we eat now?" he asked for the fifth time, leaning dramatically against the wall. "I'm wasting away."

"You had two rolls an hour ago," Ethan reminded him.

"Those were practice rolls," Oliver argued. "Athletes carb-load before the main event."

He scribbled in his log with a flourish:

B-78: Practice rolls. B-79: Training for pie Olympics.

But before anyone could sit at the table, there was one more tradition. Both Mom's and Dad's families had passed it down for years: a mini cornhole tournament in the backyard. Everyone paired up into teams. The prize? First pick of dessert.

Oliver tossed his beanbag with dramatic flair, announcing, "This shot determines the fate of the pie!" He missed the board entirely.

B-80: Missing with style.

Ethan smirked, sinking a toss right in the hole. He wrote neatly:

Blessing #29: Winning at cornhole.

Grandma surprised everyone by lobbing hers underhand— thunk! Right on the board. "Beginner's luck," she said, though the twinkle in her eye said otherwise.

Oliver shouted, "B-81: Grandma's secret cornhole skills!"

Cousins played, uncles heckled, and Grandpa kept score like it was the Olympics. At last, Dad and Uncle Mike were crowned champions. Dad bowed deeply. "Apple pie, here I come."

Oliver scribbled:

B-82: Dad winning dessert rights. B-83: Uncle Mike as pie wingman.

Finally, the table was ready: turkey golden and steaming, sourdough rolls piled high, garden carrots shining, pies waiting in the wings. Everyone gathered around, bowing their heads as Dad cleared his throat.

"Lord, today we give You thanks—for food, family, and freedom. For the laughter in this house. And for the men and women serving near and far away, standing watch so we can gather here in peace. Bless them and keep them safe."

"Amen," the family echoed.

Ethan added softly:

Blessing #30: Prayers that reach far away.

Oliver tapped his pencil and called out:

B-84: Amen chorus. B-85: Cranberry sauce still standing tall.

Then came the tradition: everyone naming one thing they were thankful for before the feast began.

"Grandma's pie," Oliver blurted.

"You're supposed to wait your turn," Ethan said.

Grandpa chuckled. "Let him go. He looks like he's going to pop if he holds it in."

Oliver stood up, pie already on his mind, but then paused. His voice wobbled between silly and serious. "Actually...I want to say a real one first. I'm thankful...for everybody putting up with my silliness. I know I'm kind of a middle-aged kid—"

"You're eight," Ethan interrupted.

"Exactly," Oliver said, pointing. "That's middle-aged in kid years. And I'm changing every day. Sometimes I don't know what to do with all my...Oliver-ness." He waved his arms dramatically, nearly knocking over the cranberry sauce. "But you guys laugh with me, not at me. So thanks. For, you know...helping me deal with being me."

For a moment, the table went quiet. Then Grandma reached over and squeezed his hand. "Sweetheart, that's one of the best blessings you could give us."

Oliver sniffed and scribbled:

B-86: Family who laughs with me, not at me. B-87: Safe place to be Oliver.

Ethan gave him a sideways grin. "You're still annoying, though."

Ethan noted carefully:

Blessing #31: A brother who's annoyingly lovable.

Oliver grinned back. "Annoyingly lovable. B-88!"

Everyone laughed, and the heaviness lifted.

Then it was Ethan's turn. He cleared his throat. "I'm thankful for this house. For the garden, and our notebooks, and for Dad teaching us about people who are far away, keeping us safe. And for Oliver, too. Even when he's...Oliver."

He wrote:

Blessing #32: This house.

Blessing #33: Our garden.

Blessing #34: Dad teaching us.

Blessing #35: Oliver (most of the time).

Oliver puffed out his chest. "See? Lovable. B-89!"

Mom added her voice next: "I'm thankful for freedom—and for faith that holds steady through every season."

Grandpa raised his glass. "For family stories that never get old."

Ethan smiled as the blessings multiplied around the table, even when they weren't numbered in his log.

Plates began to pass—turkey, carrots, mashed potatoes. Rolls disappeared faster than Grandma could butter them. The table rattled with laughter and the clatter of serving spoons.

Oliver scribbled as quickly as he ate:

B-90: Turkey drumsticks. B-91: Mashed potatoes volcano. B-92: Gravy flood. B-93: Cranberry splats. B-94: Rolls vanishing into my mouth.

When the pie finally landed in front of Oliver, he held his fork like a sword. "To battle!" he cried, and dug in with gusto.

B-95: Pumpkin pie round one. B-96: Pumpkin pie round two. B-97: Pumpkin pie victory lap.

By the end of the meal, his cheeks were stuffed and his belly round. He slumped in his chair and sighed.

B-98: Pie coma. B-99: Family who doesn't judge my pie coma.

Ethan wrote, trying not to laugh:

Blessing #36: Oliver surviving pie coma.

"*B-100: Brother writing about my pie coma,*" Oliver added weakly, patting his stomach like a drum.

The whole table erupted in laughter as the last crumbs disappeared and the house hummed with contentment.

Notebook / Conversation Prompt:

If you had to give thanks for something about yourself—something that makes you uniquely you—what would it be?

Faith Connection:

1 Thessalonians 5:18 — *Give thanks in all circumstances; for this is God's will for you in Christ Jesus.*

Chapter 6: The Blessing

"BL-ESS-

INGGGGGO"

The feast was finished, the dishes stacked high, and the house smelled of butter and cinnamon even hours later. Ethan and Oliver had already been drafted into cleanup duty—drying silverware, wiping down the table, and carrying plates until their arms ached.

At last, they collapsed onto the living room couch, notebooks in hand. Mom and Dad sat on either side, steaming mugs of coffee in their hands.

Ethan flipped open his notebook and grinned. "I'm up to Blessing #37—family, food, our garden, the people who serve away from home, even geese flying in a V."

Oliver turned his notebook around, revealing pages covered in doodles of pie slices with faces and turkeys in superhero capes. "I'm up to B-99."

Ethan frowned. "There aren't 99 pies."

"There could be," Oliver said. "If science would hurry up."

Mom laughed, her eyes twinkling. "Show me your favorite one so far."

Oliver jabbed a finger at the middle of the page. "This one: B-72—second slice of pie when no one's looking."

Dad chuckled. "That's very...Oliver."

Just then, Grandma drifted in from the kitchen, drying her hands on a towel. "What's all this?" she asked.

"Mission report," Ethan explained, holding up his notebook. "We're writing down blessings."

Grandma smiled and sank into her armchair. "Well, add one more: having grandsons who remind me to notice mine."

Uncle Josh poked his head in from the dining room, a cribbage board still set on the table behind him. "Mine is always having someone to play cards with."

Soon cousins and aunts and uncles wandered in, each offering a story, a laugh, or a memory. The living room began to glow with gratitude, brighter than any lamp.

Ethan scribbled quickly to keep up. His neat handwriting marched across the page:

Blessing #38: A family that prays and laughs together.

Oliver doodled turkeys with speech bubbles shouting blessings. Then, with a dramatic flourish, he wrote across the bottom of the page:

B-100: Being loved exactly as I am.

He leapt to his feet like a Bingo caller. "B-100! Mission complete!"

The room erupted in laughter and applause. Ethan just shook his head, smiling.

Finally, Dad leaned forward, resting his elbows on his knees. His voice was steady but gentle.

"Before we head out, let's end this day the way it deserves—by thanking God."

The room grew quiet.

Dad prayed first, thoughtful and sure:

"Lord, thank You for more than full plates. Thank You for the laughter that carried through this house, the memories we shared, and the people we love. Thank You for safe homes, for freedom, and for the men and women serving far away tonight. Watch over them, and teach us to carry grateful hearts into each new day."

Ethan's voice followed. "Thank You for the garden, for the rolls, and for being together."

Oliver squeezed his notebook shut and added, "Thanks for pie. Thanks for family. And thanks for everyone who lets me be silly—even when I don't know how to be anything else."

Mom's voice trembled, but her words were clear. "Amen."

The quiet that followed wrapped the family like a quilt. Outside, the November air was sharp and cold, but inside, hearts felt rooted and warm.

By the time the last stories were told and coffee cups drained, it was late—so late the stars scattered high above the mountains as the truck rumbled home.

In the dim dashboard glow, Ethan scrawled one last line: *Blessing #38: A Thanksgiving not to forget.*

Beside him, Oliver whispered to himself with a grin, "B-100 forever."

Operation Gratitude was a mission well accomplished.

Debriefing the Mission

Back at home, with goodnight prayers said and hugs made, the boys sat on their beds, notebooks open in the soft lamplight, their minds still buzzing from the day.

Ethan flipped to the last page where Mom had written earlier: *Debrief Questions.* He read them aloud, his voice low and steady: "What blessing surprised you most this week? Who can you thank this year, even if they aren't at your table? How can you share gratitude with others—not just today, but all year?"

He tapped his pencil thoughtfully, then began to write: *Surprised by how even small things—like bread dough rising—can feel big. I want to thank people who can't be home, like Mom's Navy friends and shipmates. I can share by praying out loud and noticing blessings every day.*

He glanced down at the bottom of his neat list, smiling as he saw his last line: *Blessing #38: A Thanksgiving not to forget.*

Across the room, Oliver sprawled on his stomach, legs kicking lazily in the air. He scribbled fast; letters lopsided and bold:

Surprised that I didn't turn into a pumpkin. I want to thank Grandma for pie and the Navy for keeping us safe. I can share by making people laugh.

Then he sat up, flipped his notebook dramatically, and pointed to the bottom of his page where he had circled it three times:

B-100: Being loved exactly as I am.

He waved the notebook in the air. "Comedy is my ministry," he declared.

Ethan laughed, shaking his head. "Actually...that's true. You do make everyone laugh and smile."

Just outside the bedroom door, Mom and Dad paused, listening. They leaned against the frame, their eyes soft and knowing. Neither wanted to break the moment—their boys' voices drifting into the hall, full of sincerity, silliness, and faith.

Inside, Ethan carefully closed his notebook. "Mission complete," he whispered.

Oliver yawned and flopped onto his pillow. "Best. Mission. Ever. B-100 forever."

Mom and Dad slipped quietly down the hall, hearts full. And though Thanksgiving Day had ended, its blessings lingered, ready to carry them into each new day.

Operation Gratitude wasn't just a Thanksgiving mission—it was an everyday one.

Commander's End of Mission Prayer:

Lord, thank You for the blessings seen and unseen, big and small.

Thank You for the smell of pies baking and bread rising, for laughter that fills a room, for stories told around the table, and for quiet moments where we remember You are with us.

We thank You for family gathered close tonight, and we thank You for the families who feel far away— those with empty seats at their tables, those who are missing moms or dads serving in the military, or working hard to keep others safe, fed, and cared for. Wrap them in Your love and remind them they are not forgotten.

Bless the men and women who stand watch this holiday, whether on ships, in the skies, or far across the world. Bless their families at home with comfort, courage, and joy until they can be together again.

Help us carry thankful hearts into each new day, not just on Thanksgiving but in every season. Teach us to notice blessings all around us—in the food we share, the friends we laugh with, the chores we do, the prayers we say, and even in the silly moments that make us smile.

Most of all, thank You for Jesus, the greatest gift we could ever receive.

Amen.

Thanksgiving Mission Log

Your mission isn't over yet! Grab a pencil and paper (or your own notebook) and write down your answers to these debrief questions:

- What blessing surprised you most this week?
- Who can you thank this year, even if they aren't at your table?
- How can you share gratitude with others — not just today, but all year?

Remember: blessings can be big or small, serious or silly. Just like Ethan & Oliver, you get to notice them all.

Example of Ethan & Oliver's Thanksgiving Mission Log

Mission Objective: Notice blessings — big ones, little ones, and even silly ones!

Blessings I Found Today

1.

2.

3.

4.

5.

My Silliest Blessing

Someone I Want to Thank (not at my table)

How I Can Share Gratitude Every Day

Mission Doodle Zone:
(Draw a blessing — pie slices, silly turkeys, or anything that made you smile today!)

Commander's Note:
Gratitude isn't just for Thanksgiving — it's an everyday mission!

Play Along at Home!

Want to join Ethan & Oliver's Blessing Bingo?
We've created a printable game where you can cross off blessings just like the boys did during *Operation Gratitude*.

Scan the QR code to download your Thanksgiving Blessing Bingo card and play along with your family this holiday season.

Who will be the first to shout...
BL-ESS-INGGO!

Or visit

Www.EthanAndOliverAdventures.com/Thanksgiving-Mission

Want more Ethan & Oliver?

Check out our blog and subscribe for bonus activities, Stop & Explore missions, recipes, and updates on new book releases heading your way!

www.EthanAndOliverAdventures.com

or scan the QR code below